T0128622

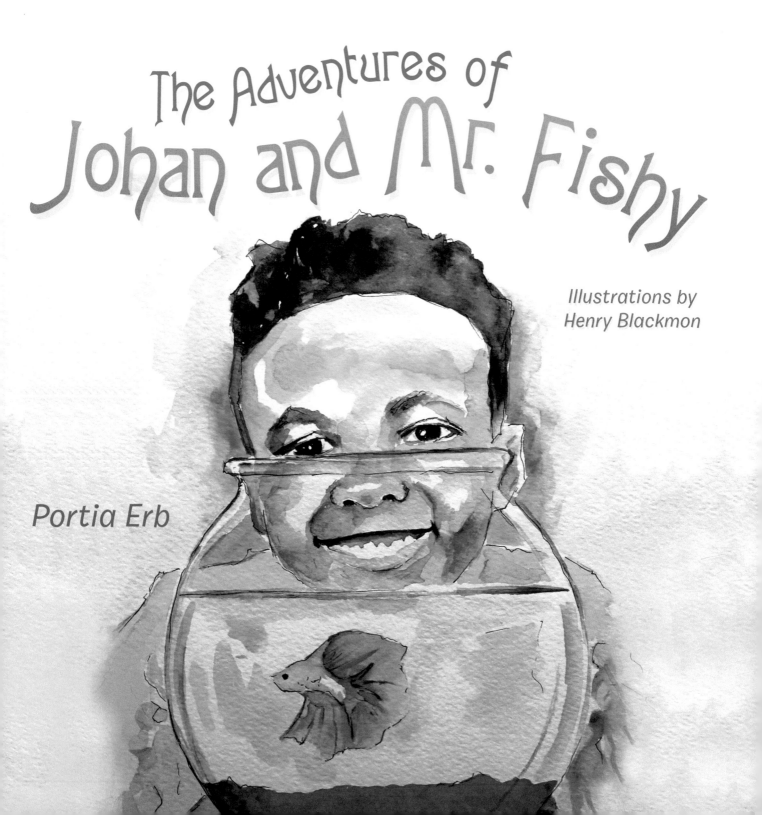

The Adventures of
Johan and Mr. Fishy

Illustrations by
Henry Blackmon

Portia Erb

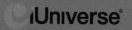

Dedication: This book is dedicated to my grandchildren Jeremiah, Johan, Kayleigh, and Kaylani who are as adventurous as they come. Fearless sometimes to a fault. Especially my grandson Johan, who lives life as one big adventure. Never taking himself too serious or others. He is always down for an adventure, and so are his siblings who will follow him in his adventures anytime, anywhere. Most of them anyway.

The Birthday Gift.

One day Johan was given a beta fish for his birthday. A gift given to him by one of his mother's friends. He named him Mr. Fishy. He was given strict instructions to observe Mr. Fishy in his fish tank, and not feed Mr. Fishy but once a day. He along with his siblings, Kayleigh, Kaylani, and Jeremiah were given strict instruction not to put their hands into the fish tank, along with the feeding instructions.

Mr. Fishy was given to Johan as a birthday gift. It was his sole responsibility to oversee the care of Mr. Fishy. Johan was so excited not only to have a pet fish, but to have the awesome responsibility of caring for a pet.

One day when his parents were busy with other responsibilities, Johan and Kayleigh decided to investigate to see how close they could get to Mr. Fishy. Johan talked Kayleigh into cleaning the fish tank. He decided the fish tank was too cloudy, and without permission, decided to take Mr. Fishy out of tank, feed him, and clean the tank. Since they were downstairs close to the bathroom, they cleaned the tank, but decided Mr. Fishy needed to be put in water during the time they were cleaning the fish tank. During Johan and Kayleigh's decision to clean the fish tank out, they poured Mr. Fishy out of the fish bowl into the toilet. What they did not know was that there was no where for Mr. Fishy to swim around, because although there is water in the toilet there is no place for it to contain Mr. Fishy, so when they put Mr. Fishy in the toilet he swam down the drain.

Kayleigh and Johan were confused. How could Mr. Fishy get away so fast? So many things went through their heads. How would they get

Mr. Fishy back? What would they tell their parents about how Mr. Fishy got out of the fish tank? Where did Mr. Fishy go? How much trouble would they get into?

Their parents returned to Johan and Kayleigh downstairs in the living room looking at each other. One pointing to the other. Kia, their mother asked, Kayleigh why are you pointing to Johan? Kayleighs' version: Kayleigh said, Johan said it would be a good idea to touch Mr. Fishy. He also said that the fish tank was dirty, and Mr Fishy looked hungry, so we could feed him, touch him, and clean the fish tank.

So we poured Mr. Fishy into the toilet, not knowing that he would go down the drain. Therefore, we did not get to touch Mr. Fishy, feed him, or clean his fish bowl, which did not need cleaning. (P.S. Mr Fishy was a birthday gift he had just received). Johan's version: Johan said to his parents that he took one look at Mr. Fishy and thought to himself. What a beautiful fish. I would love to see how Mr. Fishy is able to wiggle his tail. It would be nice to just touch him. Then I thought Mr. Fishy really really looks hungry, and I think it would be a good idea to just give Mr. Fishy some fresh water that would make his fish tank even better than it was before. Johan then shared his idea's with Kayleigh who thought all of this sounds good. (From the mouth of a 7 year old to that of a 10 year old.) They then poured Mr. Fishy into the toilet forgetting that there is no way for Mr. Fishy to stay in the bowl. He continued to swim down stream. Johan then explained that Mr. Fishy did not die, is not lost or confused. He went out to sea to join his family. So he and Kayleigh had done Mr. Fishy a good deed, because even though Mr. Fishy was no longer with them. He was with his family in the ocean or the sea. So even though Johan did not get to touch Mr. Fishy's beautiful fin's, clean out his tank, or feed him. He was ok with Mr. Fishy's departure, because he knew he was with his fish family. What logic!

Although Johan and Kayleigh appeared to be ok with this explanation of Mr. Fishy's departure, their parents were not. Johan and Kayleigh were sent to their rooms to reflect on what had just taken place. Not before their parents told them during their time in their perspective rooms to reflect on the importance of gifts being given to you, and what you do to honor the person that gave you that give, and what that really means. They both spent time in their room. Johan thinking about what Mr. Fishy was doing with his family, and not really understanding the importance of the gift that was given to him. Just hoping that he would one day see Mr. Fishy again.

Kayleigh, not so much, went to her room thinking about how she let a 7 year old talk her into taking a fish out of its tank, and allow it to swim down the drain. She vowed never to listen to Johan when it came to one of his adventures, but you will soon find out that is not true. Kayleigh remembered all of the things he had said to get her to go along with his adventure, to include: touching Mr. Fishy's fin, cleaning his fish tank, and feeding him. Not only did that not work, but now she is having to share in a punishment for someone elses birthday gift. In the word's of Kayleigh "WHY, WHY, WHY?

Mr. Fishys second chance.

Johan's aunt, London, found out about Mr. Fishys early departure, and decided she would lend a hand. She decided to purchase Johan another beta fish, along with all of the accessories to go along with his care. Her sister Brittany wanted to visit Johan and his siblings, so she rode with London to take Johan his birthday gift.

Johan was so excited to see both of his aunt's, but was thrilled that London had given him another chance at being a pet owner, with her gift of another beta fish. Johan also decided to name this fish Mr.

Fishy. This time he was also given strict instructions on how to care for the beta fish. This time when he received the fish it was placed into a plastic bag with water, so it could easily be transferred into the fish tank. Johan, Kayleigh, Kalani, and Jeremiah watched intently as Johan was given his new gift, also a birthday gift. London and Brittany stayed to visit and gave Johan instructions on how to care for Mr. Fishy. They were well aware of how Mr. Fishy made his first demise, or how he in Johan's words "joined his fish family".

Soon London and Brittany left to return to their perspective homes. Next, Johan's mother asked Johan to wait for a moment, and she would help him to transfer Mr. Fishy into the fish tank. Johans mother went into the other room, and she stayed a little too long for Johan.

During that short period of time he, Kayleigh, Kaylani, and Jeremiah discussed how beautiful the fish was, and how since Mr. Fishy was already out of the fish tank and had not been put into the fish bowl, that they all could readily touch Mr. Fishy to welcome him into the family. Jeremiah, who is the oldest sibling, said he did not want to do that, and that it was a bad idea. Kayleigh and Kaylani said they really wanted to do it, and thought it was a great idea. Remember: I told you that Johan's siblings are always down for any adventure with him except for Jeremiah, who is always the voice of reason. Jeremiah told them that they needed to wait for their mother, and he wanted nothing to do with it, and then he went to his room. Johan knew he was short on time since their mother would be back soon. He once again roped his sister Kayleigh into his mischief and adventure. Kaylani watched in amazement.

Johan asked Kayleigh to open up the plastic bag, so that they could rub Mr. Fishy like you would a puppy. Kayleigh then proceeded to open the bag but not before putting Mr. Fishy in the kitchen sink, so that they all could touch Mr. Fishy, and make him feel welcome into the family. Kayleigh was sure to make sure that she put water into the sink, and put the stopper in to contain Mr. Fishy. Each one of them took their turn touching Mr. Fishy and saying welcome. Just as they all finished touching Mr. Fishy and welcoming him into the family.

Kayleigh had her hand in the water touching Mr. Fishy and his beautiful moving fins when in walked their mother. They all screamed. Kayleigh was so startled, she accidently pulled the stopper out of the kitchen sink, and down the drain Mr. Fishy went.

Kayleigh and Kaylani were so sad, they proceeded to cry. Johan looked up and said, "Mr. Fishy has joined his brother". Johan's mother asked for an explanation of what happened to Mr. Fishy. Johan said he would be delighted to explain. He began: We tried to wait on you to come back from the other room, but you were taking too long, so we all decided to welcome Mr. Fishy. We decided that the way to do that was to take Mr. Fishy out of the bag and pet him, by touching his beautiful fins. So we decided that the best way to take turns touching Mr. Fishy would be to take him out of the plastic bag with water, and put him into the kitchen sink, and we all would be able to take turns welcoming him into the family. Johan also explained that it was just an accident, and that Mr. Fishy was not dead, he just went to join his brother along with his family, so there was no need for any type of punishment. By this time Jeremiah had come out of his room. He explained to his mother that he tried to tell them that what they were doing was not a good idea.

Johan's mother was not impressed with Johan's explanation, or the fact that Jeremiah said he told them not to do it. They all were lectured about the importance taking care of gifts that they are given, also the importance of informing their parents when a challenging situation arises. They all were sent to their rooms to reflect on what just happened to Mr. Fishy.

Reflections:

Jeremiah: In his room thinking, why am I being punished? It was not my gift. I told them not to do it, but they did it anyway. I guess I should have gone to get mom when they started talking about what they were going to do. I guess I could have prevented the demise of Mr. Fishy. Maybe, maybe not. I wonder what time I have football practice tomorrow? Hmmmm

Kayleigh: It was not my fault. It was Johan's fault. It was not my birthday gift. Poor Mr. Fishy. Am I the reason Mr. Fishy is gone? Johan roped me into his trouble again. Well like Johan said Mr. Fishy is with his brother, and with his fish family. I will not be fooled by Johan again. (Or will she?)

Kaylani: I just want to have some fun. I was just doing what my brother told me to. Why do I have to come to my room? This is for when someone gets in trouble. It is all Johan's fault. I want a snack. I am going ask mommy can I have a snack.

Johan: What a wonderful day. Although Mr. Fishy is gone. At least he is with his brother, and the rest of his family in the ocean or the sea. Life is good. I know I am suppose to be in my room reflexing(reflecting) on what I did, but I do not see what the big deal is when Mr. Fishy is with his family. I will go and tell my mom I love her. I think I will tell London I love her too, when I see her.

In Conclusion

It appears Johan does not show his appreciation for his birthday gifts. It may seem he has neglected his responsibility as a pet owner, did not follow directions from his parents or his aunts, and did not appreciate his birthday gifts. To Johan his receipt of two birthday gifts was just a way for him to display his sense of wonder and adventure. He leads his brother and sisters into his world of wonder and adventure whether they wanted to be there or not. What will be Johan's next life adventure? Will his sisters and brother follow?

THE END

Printed in the United States
by Baker & Taylor Publisher Services